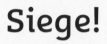

# Siege!

## by

## Ann Jungman

## Illustrated by Alan Marks

You do not need to read this page – just get on with the book!

First published in 2005 in Great Britain by
Barrington Stoke Ltd
www.barringtonstoke.co.uk

ISBN 1-842993-35-6

Printed in Great Britain by Bell & Bain Ltd

## Meet The Author – Ann Jungman

*What is your favourite animal?*
**Wolf**
*What is your favourite boy's name?*
**Guy**
*What is your favourite girl's name?*
**Abigail**
*What is your favourite food?*
**Beef stroganoff**
*What is your favourite music?*
**Bob Dylan**
*What is your favourite hobby?*
**Cinema and cooking**

## Meet The Illustrator – Alan Marks

*What is your favourite animal?*
**Snow leopard**
*What is your favourite boy's name?*
**Thomas**
*What is your favourite girl's name?*
**Kate**
*What is your favourite food?*
**Oysters**
*What is your favourite music?*
**Mozart**
*What is your favourite hobby?*
**Cooking**

For Penny and Jamie and
in memory of Paul

# Contents

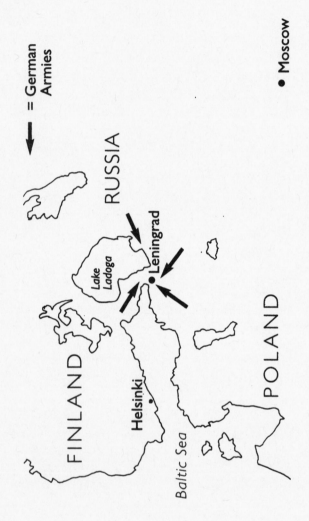

# Chapter 1
# Digging

Ivan looked out of the window and wished he was still on holiday. He loved fishing in the river and picking berries. Ivan didn't like school very much.

All at once, the door of the classroom flew open and the headmaster walked in. He was in a hurry.

"All of you, into the trucks outside," he shouted. "Your country needs you."

All the boys looked at one another, puzzled.

"What does he mean?" asked one.

"No questions," snapped the headmaster. "Into the lorry and do as you are told."

As the boys drove through the wide elegant streets of Leningrad, Ivan thought what a city it was. But the roads were much more crowded that day than usual. Lorry after lorry full of students and school children roared down the streets that were normally so peaceful. What could it mean?

Soon they'd left the city behind and were out in the countryside. The lorry came to a sudden stop.

"Everyone out," shouted their teacher. As the boys jumped down from the lorry, a Russian soldier came towards them.

"Everyone grab one of those spades and follow me!" he yelled. "Move it!"

Ivan ran after him.

"What's happening?" he panted. "What are we doing out here?"

"Didn't they tell you?" asked the soldier.

Ivan shook his head. "No-one knows," he said.

"Hitler has invaded Russia," the soldier said and spat on the side of the road. "Yesterday the Germans crossed the Russian border like robbers in the night. There was no warning. They didn't declare war. They just started their bombing and killing."

"But Comrade Stalin, our great leader, made a pact with Hitler that we wouldn't invade Germany and they wouldn't invade us," said Ivan.

"Yes, well for pigs like Hitler pieces of paper don't mean anything. They sign them when they feel like it and then they tear them up later. All right, boys! Stop here and start digging."

Ivan took a deep breath and started to dig. All around were people digging. Most were young but some older people were there as well, all using the spades as if there was no tomorrow.

"What are we digging?" asked a girl.

"Tank traps," the soldier said in a grim voice. "Big trenches that the German tanks won't be able to cross."

"Tanks," said Ivan. "But the Germans will never get this far, will they? We're hundreds of miles from the border."

"Yes, well, better safe than sorry," the soldier went on, "We didn't know they were going to attack us. Our armies aren't ready and may not be able to stop the Germans. They may easily get as far as this. We need to be good and ready for them. Dig in groups of ten and don't waste energy talking. Just dig. Then dig some more."

Ivan and his friends dug and dug. Soon they were dripping with sweat and big blisters had developed on their hands.

All around, other groups were digging in the same determined way. They weren't talking or looking around but just kept on at the job. Ivan looked up and was amazed to see his sister Varya with a spade in her hand.

Princess Varya, his stuck-up sister, was doing something useful with her hands for once. Varya was a prize pupil at the most famous music school in Leningrad. She played the piano and always had to keep her hands dry and soft. She could never even wash a cup. Ivan grinned. *Oh well*, he thought, *this war isn't all bad*.

"Hey, Varya," he shouted. "What are you doing here? You'll have to soak your hands for at least six hours after this."

"Don't talk rubbish," his sister shouted back. She was angry. "All Russians have got to help in any way they can. Look – even my teacher, Shostakovich, is here, digging like the rest of us."

Ivan gasped. Shostakovich was the most famous composer and pianist in all of Russia and here he was with a spade. This was a bit different from piano playing. Things must be bad.

# Chapter 2
# Alone

They drove back to Leningrad as the sun was setting. Water sparkled on the canals. You were never far from water in Leningrad. The city had been built on marshes and you could never forget it. The Baltic Sea was on one side and huge Lake Ladoga on the other.

Ivan and Varya staggered up the steps of their flat. They were worn out and dirty and their hands were covered in blisters. At the top of the stairs stood their father in his army uniform.

"Thank goodness," he called to them, "I was waiting for you. I have to go back to the army but I didn't want to go without saying goodbye."

All the colour left Varya's face.

"Will you be gone a long time?" Ivan asked. He was worried.

"No, of course not," his father said. "We'll have those Germans back across the border in no time."

Ivan didn't believe him. How often had he heard his father whispering to his mother at night? He said that their Great Leader, Stalin, had got rid of all the best generals.

"As soon as someone shows he's good or his men like him, Stalin gets jealous and has him shot," his father had said.

"Wish your old dad luck, then," said his father and they held onto each other hard in a big hug.

"Don't look so worried. The Germans won't win. If we can hold out till winter, there are two famous generals waiting for Hitler and his armies."

Ivan gave a grin. "You mean General Frostbite and General Hunger will get them."

"That's right, son, and don't you forget it. We Russians know how to deal with the cold in a way others don't. Just remember how we've always defeated invaders in the past. All those armies that tried to take over Russia, the French, the Germans, they've all had to turn back. No-one can defeat us on our home ground – it may take time but we'll win in the end. Just think about that and hold onto it, whatever happens.

"Now come on, I want to take a photo of my family, so I can look at you whenever I want."

Ivan and Varya got washed and then sat with their mother and little Sasha while their father took some photos. Two-year-old Sasha made everyone laugh by pulling his mother's hair.

"Now let me take one of you, Dad," cried Ivan and he grabbed the camera. "Then we can look at you whenever we want too."

Ivan took a photo of them all in front of the window.

Then their father put on his greatcoat and his fur hat and went to the door. He hugged and kissed their mother and little Sasha, and then Ivan and Varya.

"Look after your mother and Sasha. I'm counting on you both."

"Don't worry, Dad, we will," Ivan said in a firm voice. Then his father ran down the stairs and jumped into a waiting truck.

They all rushed to the window to wave to him.

"I wonder if we'll ever see him again," their mother said softly and kissed Sasha on the top of his head.

"Of course we will," shouted Varya. "We will, I know we will and we'll crush that horrible Hitler too."

"I do hope you're right," said her mother with a sigh. "Now, I'm sorry but you two are going to have to look after Sasha tonight. I'm on night duty. All doctors have to report to the hospital. There's some food in the kitchen. I'll be back to look after Sasha in the morning, before you go to school."

After she left, Varya and Ivan looked at each other.

"What a day," she said. "First we dig ditches all day and then both our parents have to go off and abandon us."

"I know," agreed Ivan. "It all feels very odd but something tells me it's going to get worse."

# Chapter 3
# The Siege

Things moved very fast in the next few weeks. German planes often flew low over Leningrad on bombing raids. German guns kept shelling the city. The noise was horrible. Ivan and Varya didn't see their mother much. She was busy at the hospital. She had to look after the hundreds of wounded soldiers who came in from the front. Most nights she slept at work, if she got any sleep at all. Soon there was no more school and their old life was gone.

One day their mother came home, pale and worn out.

"There's going to be a siege. Hitler's made up his mind to take the city," she said.

"A siege!" cried Ivan. "But sieges happened in the Middle Ages. There were battering rams and people poured boiling oil from the ramparts and city walls. That's not modern war."

"Well, the Germans are going to set up camp all round Leningrad and starve us out," their mother told him grimly.

"No way," cried Ivan. "They'll never win. I'd rather die than give in to them."

"Me too," agreed Varya.

"Sasha too," said their little brother, nodding.

They all laughed, glad for something to smile about.

"Children, you need to listen to me and think hard about what I have to say," said their mother. "Most of the children and some of the very important people are being taken out of Leningrad. I can't go. They need all the doctors to stay here. But you *could* go. I've got places for you on the transport trucks."

"What about Sasha?" Ivan wanted to know.

"You must take him too," said their mother. She sounded very tired.

"We can't leave you here alone. We must stick together, Mum. I'm staying with you. Varya can take Sasha to safety."

"If you think I'm going and leaving you here, you'd better think again," snapped Varya. "I could have gone with my teacher, Shostakovich. He begged me to leave with him, but I said no. I'm not going now, just because you asked me to take Sasha."

"Please, Varya," begged her mother.

"No, Ivan and I will look after Sasha and fight for our city if we have to."

"Things will get very bad," warned their mother. "If they bomb the power stations there will be no heat. The food has almost run out and the bombing and shelling will get worse."

"We've made up our minds, Mum. There's no more to say," smiled Ivan. "Now, you look tired out. Let me make you a cup of tea and then you must sleep for a bit."

Their mother began to smile.

*All at once, my children have grown up – it's a shock but a nice one*, she thought.

Their mother was right. Things did get worse. Winter came and the temperature fell below freezing. Just as she said, the power stations were bombed and there was no light and no heating. Life was now all about staying alive.

Varya found a few candles for light and Ivan went out and collected bits of wood from bombed buildings. Everyone else was doing the same and Ivan got into lots of fights.

One freezing night Varya was hugging a cold and sad Sasha. "We'd better burn some of Father's books," she said.

"Varya, are you mad? Father would never forgive you."

"Of course he would. Look at Sasha. His teeth are chattering. Go and get some books, the big thick ones. They'll burn well and not too fast. And while you're at it, bring some of my music. We'll burn that too, to warm us up a bit."

"But, Varya, your music is the most important thing in your life."

"The most important thing in my life is that we all stay alive. You must do what I say. I'll tell Dad why we had to burn his books when the war is over."

Ivan thought about the Varya he had known before the war.

"I remember when a broken finger nail seemed like the worst thing in the world to you," he teased. "I used to think you were a spoilt brat. I was wrong," he said.

Varya smiled.

********

That night Ivan stood on the roof of their block of flats and watched out for firebombs. Everyone from the flats took it

in turns to keep watch. The planes roared overhead and a bomb came down. Ivan rushed to get it and then dropped it in a bucket of water. He walked up and down stamping his feet and rubbing his hands to keep them warm. He tried not to think about how hungry he was.

*I hate all Germans*, he thought to himself. *If it wasn't for them our family would be together, and I wouldn't be freezing cold and hungry and bored and scared. I hate every single German in the world. I want to kill as many as I can.*

Then Ivan smelled something wonderful. It wasn't the usual smell of burning and bombs. It smelled delicious. Ivan's mouth watered. He looked out to see a huge fire ablaze in the middle of the city.

Ivan saw that the main food warehouse was on fire. That was where most of the food in Leningrad was kept. The food warehouse had been bombed. The delicious smell made his hunger even more painful. Ivan knew it was the last of the city's store of food for the winter going up in flames.

*Now we'll starve, as well as freeze*, thought Ivan grimly. Another firebomb dropped and Ivan picked it up and threw it into the bucket. *But we won't give in, no, we'll never give in.*

# Chapter 4
# Hunger

The weeks passed and nothing got any better. After the bombing of the food warehouse there was less and less to eat.

"I'm hungry all the time," moaned Ivan.

"Everyone is," snapped his sister. "A slice of bread a day isn't enough for anyone."

"It isn't even proper bread," Ivan went on. "It's got sawdust and mice droppings in it. No-one cares as long as we get *something*."

"We get as much as anyone else," Varya pointed out. "Only the workers in the factories and the soldiers get more than us."

Sasha began to wail. "Sasha hungry," he moaned.

Ivan and Varya looked at one another. Varya picked Sasha up and hugged him.

She was now so weak and hungry that she could hardly lift him at all.

"Hungry!" Sasha went on crying.

"Ivan, start stripping the wallpaper off the wall," Varya said.

"What are you talking about, Varya? Even if we put that in the stove it'll only burn for a minute."

"We're not going to burn it. We need to boil it up to make some soup for Sasha. I've heard there's goodness in the glue."

"Glue soup," sniffed Ivan. "It sounds disgusting."

"Don't complain," replied his sister. "It might save our lives. Go and make up a fire with Mum's medical books and I'll take this pot and go up onto the roof. I'll get some snow and melt it to make the glue soup."

When Varya returned with the snow, she said, "Your belt, Ivan. I need it for the soup."

"You can't have my belt. My trousers will fall down."

"Use this bit of scarf to keep your trousers up. I need your belt. We'll boil that too, to get some of the fat out of the leather."

That night they all sat round and ate the soup Varya had made. She put their last onion in as well. They dipped their bread into the soup and ate everything up. They began to feel a bit better. Sasha stopped crying and fell asleep. Ivan tried not to

think of his mother's dumplings and red cabbage and roast pork. He'd not eaten food that tasted good in a long time.

"Masha and Andrei upstairs have been eating rats and cats," Ivan told Varya.

"I know, but they still look skinny and ill," Varya said.

"We all look skinny and ill," agreed Ivan. "We're a city of skeletons. I'm on fire duty on the roof again tonight. Shall I go and look for some wood before I go?"

"Yes, please. You can take the sledge."

So Ivan went out into their street but it didn't look the same anymore. Once there had been tall, grand houses and shops. Now there were broken walls and holes in the road. Where the trams had once run, there was only silence and rubble. Lying here and

there were the bodies of people who had died of hunger in the streets as they went looking for food. One boy had fallen over, dead, with a pile of wood beside him. Ivan searched through the boy's pockets for his ration book and then picked up the wood. The punishment for stealing a ration book was death but Ivan didn't care. All he wanted was to help poor little Sasha.

As he walked home along the freezing street, Ivan hoped that someone would come and fetch the bodies in the morning. Now that there were so many deaths, the bodies often just lay where they fell for days.

*It's amazing*, Ivan thought to himself, *any other city would have given in but we just keep on going, no matter how many people die.*

# Chapter 5
# Sasha

Ivan was just walking up the stairs dragging the sledge with the wood behind him, when, all at once, a few lights went on.

*Electricity*, thought Ivan, *I'd forgotten what it was like*. Slowly he pushed open the door of their flat.

"I got us wood," Ivan told Varya. "I found it by a dead boy."

"Did you take his ration book?" asked Varya in a stern voice.

"Yes," said Ivan. "I don't care! If it means helping Sasha, I'll do anything."

"Give it to me," Varya said firmly. Ivan handed it to her. Varya threw it into the stove and said grimly, "Don't ever do that again, Ivan. I need you. No more crazy risks."

"How come the electricity is on?" asked Ivan.

"Masha upstairs told me that they've been working all day to get it to work so that we can all listen to the radio and hear the new music that Shostakovich has written about us."

"Your old teacher has written some music about us?" asked Ivan.

"Yes, it's called the *Leningrad Symphony*. It will tell the world how brave we are to hold out in this siege. The whole of Russia will be listening and now we can hear the music too."

Varya filled the stove with wood and turned on the radio. The three children sat close together. They put on all the clothes they had and listened to the radio.

"This is the first time this new work has been played," said the voice on the radio. "It's by our greatest composer, Comrade Shostakovich. This symphony has been written for the brave people of Leningrad. The work is called the *Leningrad Symphony*. People of Leningrad – all of Russia salutes you."

As the children listened they could hear in the music, the driving snow, the frost, the constant shelling and gunfire and the bombing. They could hear walls crashing to the ground, but they could also hear the bravery of the people of Leningrad – a city that would not give in.

"If you had left when you had the chance, Varya," Ivan said, "you could be playing with that orchestra. Do you ever wish you'd gone?"

"No," said Varya. "No, I mean, how could I have left you all? I only regret that I can't play that wonderful music."

"Sasha liked the music too," Ivan went on. "Look – he's fast asleep."

Varya smiled down at the child and stroked his pale cheek. Then she stopped.

"Ivan, Sasha is cold as ice."

Ivan picked Sasha up. His body was limp and his head flopped back.

"He's dead," said Ivan in a shaky voice. "He's died, Varya."

"Poor little Sasha," sobbed Varya. "He was so hungry and cold." The two of them held onto each other and cried and cried.

# Chapter 6
# Captured

"We must tell Mother," said Varya.

"We can't," said Ivan. "How can we get a message to her? Nothing works anymore. There are no trams, nothing. And we can't walk to the hospital. It's too far, we're too weak and it's too dangerous. The bombs are falling all the time. What are we going to do with Sasha's body? There's no-one left to come and take the bodies away and bury them."

"Even if there was," said Varya grimly, "I don't want him to be buried in this ruin of a city that is so full of pain and anger and hatred. I want our Sasha to be somewhere peaceful and beautiful."

"There's nowhere like that anymore in Leningrad," said Ivan. "But if we took him to our old summerhouse, outside the city, then we could bury his body there, under the tree where he loved to play."

"Maybe we could take him there at night," Varya said. "The summerhouse is in no-man's land. It lies between us and the German army and it's close by."

"But how can we get out at night? No-one's allowed to be out," Ivan said.

"Who'd see us?" said Varya. "There's not many people left, so many are sick or dead and as for the rest, no-one has any energy. No-one would bother."

At midnight the two set off. They pulled Sasha's small body on the sledge. They'd wrapped him up in his old blanket. They walked slowly because they had so little energy. At the end of a street they saw a Russian soldier on guard.

"We'll slip through that empty warehouse," said Ivan, "then he won't see us."

They waited until the guard moved and then crept out towards the edge of the city. They reached the countryside at last and they found their summerhouse. It had been bombed and was a ruin.

"Look," said Varya, "the tree is still standing. We'll bury Sasha there." She picked up his small body and they began to walk over to the tree.

Just then, they heard the tramping of boots. A torch shone in their faces.

"Hands up!" came a harsh voice. There were five German soldiers, all pointing their guns at the two children. Ivan put both his hands up but Varya couldn't because she was still holding Sasha.

One soldier pressed his gun into Varya's back but she still wouldn't drop Sasha.

"What have you got there?" shouted one of the soldiers in German. "Are you smugglers or is that a bomb?"

Ivan didn't understand a word but Varya replied in German.

"No, we are not smugglers, and this isn't a bomb. It's our baby brother. He's dead and we wanted to bury him under the tree where he liked to play. This used to be our summerhouse."

"They must be spies," said one of the Germans. "How else would that girl know German?"

"I know German," replied Varya, "because I am a music student and I learnt German so that I could sing German songs."

Ivan was shaking with fear. How could Varya stay so calm and answer the questions so well?

"Show me your bundle," ordered the German.

Without a word, Varya handed him the bundle.

"They're telling the truth," said the soldier. "There's a little boy in here and he's dead."

# Chapter 7
# The Enemy

"How did the child die?" asked one of the soldiers.

"We don't know," Varya told them. "We've been so cold and there's no food. We are all weak and ill. There are thousands, tens of thousands like him."

"Where is it you want to bury your brother?" asked a soldier.

"There, under that tree where he used to play. We used to have all our summer holidays here."

"What's going on?" hissed Ivan, who was still very scared. "Are they going to shoot us?"

"I don't think so," Varya told him.

The German soldiers got into a group and talked. Then one of them walked over to Varya and Ivan. He looked as if he was the officer in charge.

"We are very sad about what happened to your brother," the officer said. "We are not happy that children are getting killed and dying like this. If you let us, we would like to help you bury him out here."

"They want to help us," Varya told her brother. "They say they're upset that a little boy like Sasha died because of the siege."

"Then why don't they lift the siege and go home?" shouted Ivan angrily.

"What's he saying?" the officer asked Varya.

"He says if you're so upset about Sasha, why don't you just go home to Germany?"

"You think we don't want to? I have a child just the same age as your dead brother.

"Maybe my child is dead too. Germany is being bombed by the British. Do you think I like freezing out here month after month? Most of us are here because they forced us to join the German army. If we run away and try to make our way home, we'll be shot."

Varya looked into the man's blue eyes. She could see he was telling the truth. He and his men hated the war just as much as she and Ivan did. They were longing to go home. And she knew that if any of his men reported what had been said the officer would be shot. He was a brave man.

"I understand," she told him. "The war is terrible for us all."

She turned back to Ivan. "They're going to help us bury Sasha. The officer has a son the same age as Sasha and I think he feels sorry for us and bad about the siege."

Two of the soldiers went away and came back with spades. They dug a hole under Sasha's tree.

"Why did you pick this place to bury him?" asked the officer. "You shouldn't have left the city. You've put yourselves in great danger."

"When people die in Leningrad there's no-one left to bury them. If they are buried, the bodies are thrown into big pits with all the other dead people. We wanted Sasha to be somewhere quiet and beautiful, where he can feel the wind and hear the birds singing. He loved the woods."

"Do you know that famous German lullaby by Brahms?" asked the officer.

"Of course," Varya said.

"Would you like us all to sing that as we bury your brother? Then his spirit can be free and happy in the woods when all the fighting is over."

Varya told Ivan what the officer had said, "They want to sing a German song for Sasha, so that his spirit can rest in peace. What do you think?"

Ivan nodded, "OK. Sasha always loved singing, he'd like that."

"I'll sing in German with you," said Varya to the soldiers. "Ivan will just hum along with us." They dug a grave for Sasha and laid his body in it. While two of the soldiers put the earth in over him, the others sang. As they sang, tears ran down Varya's and Ivan's faces. When they looked up, they saw that some of the German soldiers were crying too.

*If Germans can make music like that*, thought Ivan, *they can't be all bad*.

# Chapter 8
# A Surprise

"What are you going to do with us now?" asked Varya. "If you're going to kill us, please bury us next to our brother."

"No more talk of death and killing," said the officer. "Just go back in secret."

All at once, Ivan's legs felt so weak he couldn't stand up any more. He flopped onto the ground. Varya was very weak too. She sat down next to the tree.

"You're starving, aren't you?" said the officer. He shouted to his men. "Here, all of you, give these children what food you have."

Soon Ivan and Varya had a bit of bread and sausage to eat. One of the soldiers gave them some hot coffee. Ivan had never tasted anything so good. Slowly he felt his legs getting a little stronger.

"Can you walk back to Leningrad now?" asked the officer.

Ivan nodded. He began to walk away, then he turned round and held out his hand to the officer. "Thank you for helping us," he said. "When this war is over, I hope we can be friends."

Varya told the German officer what Ivan had said. The officer smiled and they shook hands. Then Ivan and Varya walked away. The dawn was breaking as, at last, they got back to their flat.

"No-one saw us," said Varya. They fell onto their beds and were asleep at once.

A few hours later they woke up to hear someone banging on the door.

Ivan staggered and opened the door. It was hard to get up but he crawled to the door and opened it slowly. There stood a Russian army officer.

Ivan's heart sank. Had someone found out what they had done the night before? And reported them?

"I have come to speak to Comrade Varya," said the officer loudly.

"She's asleep," Ivan told him.

"Well, when she wakes up tell her she must go to the concert hall."

"How can she? The concert hall was bombed out months ago."

"That's right. It has been bombed but even so we're going to have a concert. We're going to play the *Leningrad Symphony*. We need Comrade Varya to play the piano."

"But she hasn't played the piano for so long ..."

"No-one's played any music for a long time but I've been told to find every musician in Leningrad who's still alive. They must all be at the hall by 4 p.m."

"She'll be there," promised Ivan.

# Chapter 9
# The Concert

Varya brushed her hair and put on her best dress. Then she put on her coat and gloves and big boots as well. Together, Ivan and Varya walked through the bombed streets to the concert hall. Outside the hall, they saw their mother. She looked grey and worn out and so thin. The two children ran up to her and hugged and kissed her.

"Sasha?" she asked them. "Where is Sasha?"

Varya and Ivan couldn't answer.

"I know. He's dead," said their mother in a sad small voice. "Like so many others."

"We did our best, truly we did," Ivan told her.

"I know," said his mother. She was crying now. "I know how much you both loved him."

"We've buried him in the woods near the summerhouse," Varya told her mother. "That was where he loved to be and he can listen to the birds."

"That makes me feel better. Come on, Varya. The other doctors at the hospital said I could come here today to listen to you play. Let's go in, my clever child. You play so well."

Inside the broken-down hall there were crowds of people. Most of them looked like scarecrows, pale and thin and hardly alive. There was only half an orchestra there and when the conductor came in, Ivan saw that his hands were shaking from cold and hunger.

Most of the musicians were soldiers who'd come in from the fighting for the concert. Some of them had even come from the hospital and had bandages on their legs or heads. They all looked hungry and dirty. Even so, when the concert started, everyone sat up. The music sounded strong and brave. The orchestra put all their hopes and fears into their playing. Ivan felt his spirits rise. Before, when he'd gone to hear Varya play the piano, he had been bored but this was different. Here were people, half-dead in a ruined city and still able to make music. Ivan's heart was full of pride for the people of Leningrad.

# Chapter 10
# The Ice Road

As they sat in the concert hall and listened to the music, Ivan held his mother's hand. She wept silently.

Then he felt someone tap him on the back.

"We need more men to defend the city. So many of our men are here at the concert. Can you take a gun and help defend Leningrad?"

61

Ivan nodded. He gripped his mother's hand before he left.

"I have to go, Mother, they need me to help defend the city."

His mother nodded. "I'm very proud of you, I'm very proud of you and Varya," she said.

Ivan took the gun and followed the soldier out onto the battered streets.

*At last*, he thought, *at last I'm going to be able to do my bit to save Leningrad. And I'm going to kill as many of those Germans as I can.*

But then he thought of the officer who had helped them bury Sasha and the men who had sung round the grave as they worked.

*We've got to win this war*, he thought. *We must. But after that I'll find those men. If we get through this awful war, maybe together we can make a better world.*

Ivan followed the soldier into a house and up some stairs.

"See over there," said the soldier, "that's where the Germans are. You must try and shoot as many as you can." Ivan looked out and saw the German army line up all round Leningrad. Only the lake was still and empty. Nothing moved on the ice.

All at once, far in the distance, out on the lake, he saw some trucks moving.

"Look over there, those trucks, what are they?" Ivan asked.

The soldier took out his binoculars and looked out to where Ivan was pointing. He stopped, then he said, "Those trucks are *ours*, boy. They're our trucks and they're full of supplies – food, lad, food and guns for us. Our lads have got through at last."

"How?" asked Ivan.

"They're coming across the frozen lake. We call it the Ice Road. When the ice is thick enough, lorries can drive across it from the far side where there are no

German troops. But it's very risky. They're bringing us food and help and they can take the sick and starving people away.

"Come on, lad, look through the binoculars. You'll see them. Trucks, all loaded with food and they're all flying the Russian flag.

"We're going to win through, lad, we're going to win. General Frostbite and General

Hunger will really start to attack the Germans now. They can't sit around for ever, not with our winters."

Watching the trucks coming in from the dangerous drive over the ice, Ivan knew it was true. Leningrad was going to survive. He and Varya and his mother were still alive. Maybe his father was alive too.

Leningrad was in ruins. Half the people were dead, the houses and shops were rubble, but the spirit of the city lived on. *Cities can be rebuilt*, Ivan thought. Leningrad would rise again.

Barrington Stoke would like to thank all its readers for commenting on the manuscript before publication and in particular:

Shane Allen

Oliver Baboolal

Amy Burton

Mrs P. Ely

Mrs J. Gooch

Nicholas Grimwood

Rachel Hall

Olivia Hunter

Lucia d'Inverno

Mr Klimcke

Alexander Latcham Ford

Mrs S Leszczynski

Joe Lightfoot

Emma Millburn

Nina Millburn

Alex Morter

Catherine O'Neill

Luke O'Neill

Mrs Marguerite Palmer

Ellie Pryor

Adam Roche

Edel Roche

Conor Ross

Helena Scott

Justin Stevenson

Catherine Thomson

Mrs L. Tobert

Devon Turner

Greta Walker

Gwen Waller

Rosie Simpson

## Become a Consultant!

Would you like to give us feedback on our titles before they are published? Contact us at the email address below – we'd love to hear from you!

info@barringtonstoke.co.uk
www.barringtonstoke.co.uk

# More books by Ann Jungman!

# Resistance

ISBN 1-842990-47-0

Do you ever disagree with your parents?
Jan is ashamed when his Dutch father sides
with the Germans during the Second World
War.  No-one will talk to him at school.
Only Eli is his friend.

Can Jan find a way to defy his father
and help the Resistance?

**You can order *Resistance* directly from our
website at www.barringtonstoke.co.uk**

# More exciting BRAND NEW titles!

## Robin Hood All At Sea
## by Jan Mark

Do you ever wish your life was a little more exciting? Robin Hood is Britain's **Most Wanted** outlaw. He dares to rob the rich and give to the poor. For most of us, this would be plenty of excitement – but for Robin, well, it's all as stale as last week's fish. So he sets off to sea to begin a new life – as a fisherman! But it isn't all plain sailing. Dive into this book to find out why!

**You can order *Robin Hood All At Sea* directly from our website at www.barringtonstoke.co.uk**

# More exciting
# BRAND NEW titles!

# Pet School
# by Jenny Oldfield

Bad, mad and hard to handle. And that's just Laura's mate Zoë. Their puppies are worse. At puppy training school, Laura's pup is bottom of the class. But both Laura and Zoë have other things on their minds. Like the very cute Ben and his crazy dog Shep. Will Ben ask Laura out? Or will Zoë get her paws on him first?

More exciting
BRAND NEW titles!

The Jungle House
and
The Snake Who Came to
Stay
by Julia Donaldson

ISBN 1-842993-33-X

# The Jungle House

A tiger in the back garden? A bird-eating spider in the cupboard? Welcome to the world of Elmo and his sister! Step inside the Jungle House to find out more ...

# The Snake Who Came to Stay

Polly has set up a pet's holiday home for the summer. "All creatures great and small welcome" the ad said. Her homemade zoo is getting bigger by the day ... and her mum is getting more and more fed up! Greedy guinea pigs, pesky parrots, slithering snakes. Where will it all end?

You can order *The Jungle House* directly from our website at www.barringtonstoke.co.uk